WAYNE ANDERSON'S

HORRORBLE BOOK

Come into the graveyard, where all is deadly still.

No ghost, no gremlin, no ghoul, no goblin,
nobody stirs.

Suddenly the ground opens with
a thunderous crack.
"Who's there?" you shout into
the gaping earth.

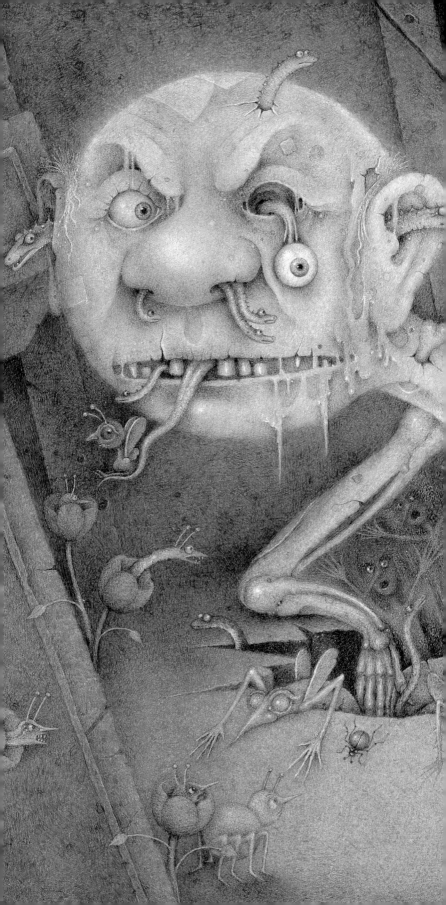

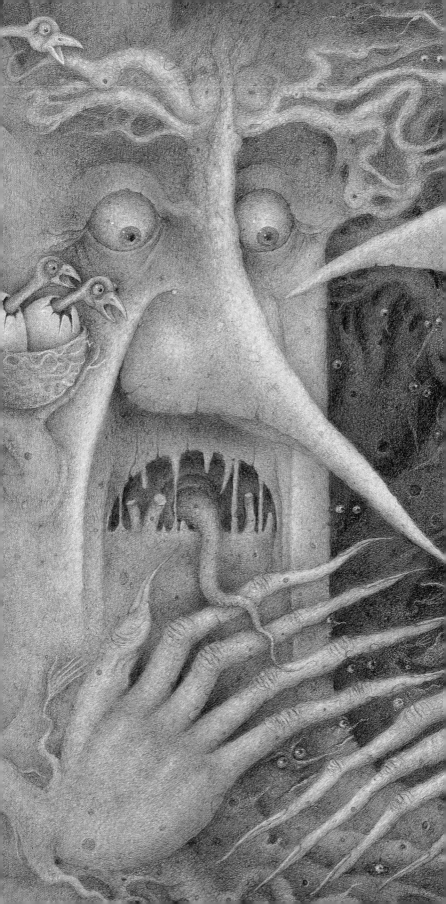

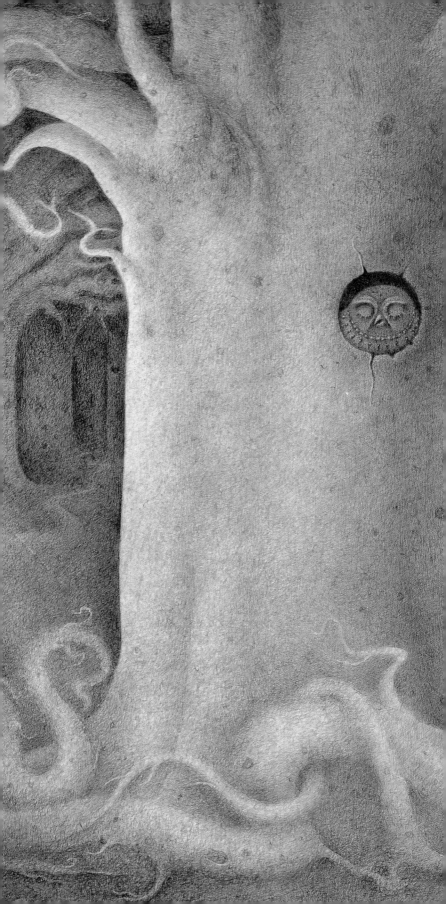

"No Body!" comes the unearthly reply.
Then the scrapyard grumbles with
gaskets and gears, "It had no body,
but it has pilfered our pipes and
snatched our springs!"
Through the clatter you hear
a distant splashing.

You follow the noise to the scrapyard.
"Who's there?" you shout
into the mountains of metal.

"*No Body!*" comes the unearthly reply.
And out of the black hole slithers a
creature that truly has no body, just
a head and arms and some bits and
pieces it has stolen from the graves.

The creature vanishes into the nearby forest. Soon there is the sound of someone chopping wood. **"Who's there?"** you shout into the night shadows.

"No Body!" comes the unearthly reply.
Then the voices of the forest scream,
"It had no body, but it has stolen
our limbs!"
In the distance there's the sound
of clanging metal.

You follow the noise to the swamp.
"Who's there?" you shout into
the watery world.

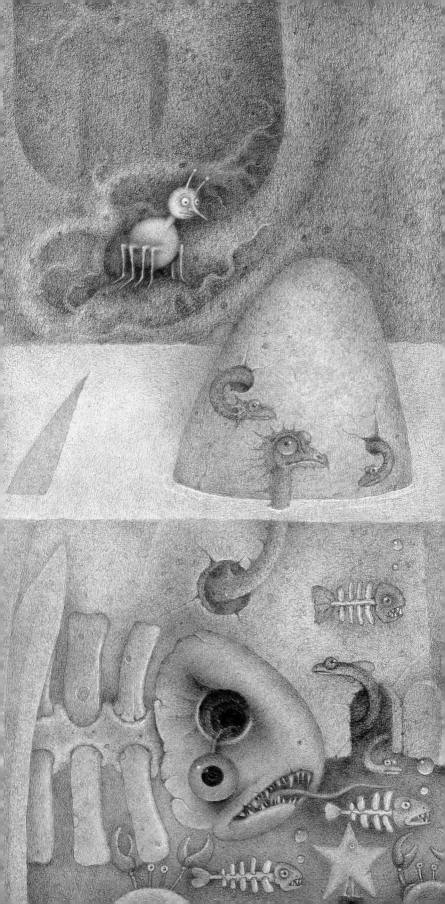

"*No Body!*" comes the unearthly reply.
Then all the underwater creatures
bubble, "It had no body, but it has
made off with our fins and skins,
our scales and tails!"

Finally, you come to a cave. All is silent. Have you imagined everything? You shout, **"Is anybody there?"**

"Not just Any Body,"
comes the distant reply.
Then the cave echoes with
squeaks and shrieks, "It has wood
and metal, fins and skin, and bits
and pieces from the graveyard.
It's building itself a real body...."

From far inside the deepest tunnel
of the cave, infernal noises grow
louder as you move closer.
"Is somebody there?" you shout.
"Yes," comes the all too earthly reply.

"Some Body is here and ready to meet you...."